THIS BOOK BELONGS TO:

_____

_____

_____

meomi

WOULD LIKE TO DEDICATE THIS BOOK TO OCTO-FANS AROUND THE WORLD AND HERMIT CRABS WITH ANEMONE HATS

MEOMI is the creative team of Vicki Wong and Michael C. Murphy who live in Vancouver, Canada with their many sasquatch friends. They enjoy writing silly stories, drinking tea, and drawing strange creatures. Meomi's art and animation has been featured in books, toys and projects worldwide. Visit them at: www.meomi.com

THAT'S AXELOTL GOOD READING IF YOU ASK ME!

MORE OCTONAUTS BOOKS:

First published in hardback in the USA by Immedium Inc. in 2009
First published in paperback in Great Britain by HarperCollins Children's Books in 2011

10 9 8 7 6 5 4 3 2

ISBN: 978-0-00-743187-8

HarperCollins Children's Books is a division of HarperCollins Publishers Ltd.

Text and illustrations copyright © MEOMI Design Inc.: Vicki Wong and Michael C. Murphy 2009

Published by arrangement with Immedium Inc. ⚙ immedium www.immedium.com

Edited by Don Menn
Design by Meomi and Stefanie Liang

Ghosts need friends, too.

THE OCTONAUTS

& the Great Ghost Reef

· MEOMI ·

HarperCollins *Children's Books*

It was a clear and sunny day under the tropical sea when...

Captain Barnacles Bear was testing his snorkel.

Peso Penguin was shampooing Clawdius.

Tunip the Vegimal was packing a picnic basket.

Dashi Dog was picking out sunglasses.

Tweak Bunny was changing a spark plug.

Dr Shellington was modelling his new swimsuit.

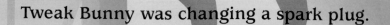

Kwazii Kitten was taking a catnap.

Professor Inkling was studying his travel guide.

The crew quickly assembled in the Octopod's headquarters to find Professor Inkling frantically pointing to the eerie landscape outside.

"Octonauts!" the small Dumbo octopus exclaimed.
"We're all excited about our holiday to the Great Reef City, but something peculiar has transpired."

"Well, shiver me timbers – everything is white,"
Kwazii puzzled out loud. "This place looks like a ghost town!"

"This city is built on top of a giant coral reef. Normally reefs look like colourful rocks where many plants and animals make their homes," Dr Shellington informed the crew. "This is not at all what I expected!"

"We need to find out what happened here," Captain Barnacles decided.

The crew cautiously explored the silent streets of the city.
As they passed abandoned buildings and empty houses,
they caught glimpses of pale shapes and heard strange creaks and moans.

"I'm sure there's a perfectly good scientific explanation for all this!" Shellington said nervously.

Eventually, they came upon an old turtle nudging a large trunk out of his front door.
Noticing the name on the mailbox, Barnacles politely asked,
"Excuse me, Mr Slowstache? Could you tell us what happened here?"
The turtle slowly looked the polar bear up and down, then gave a low sigh.

"I'm afraid it's all a great mystery." Mr Slowstache began his tale.

"When I first moved here
as a young whippersnapper,
the reef was famous for its bright colours
and seagrass aplenty to eat.

As time went by, more
and more animals came here to live.
They built fancy buildings, theatres and shops.
This place was quite the hot spot!

I guess everyone was so busy that no one noticed the coral beneath the city had started turning white and brittle. Bit by bit it spread..."

The turtle gestured sadly to his own home. "Now, even my house is falling over!

Nobody knows what caused this. Some even say the city is haunted!! I'm the last to go – it's just too cold here for my old bones."

Dashi patted the turtle's shell and asked, "Is there anything we can do to help?"

THANK YOU!

Mr Slowstache smiled in appreciation. "Thank you, young lady. I remember
a beach from my childhood just two shakes of a turtle's tail from here.
I could certainly use a hand moving my rock collection there."

The Octonauts packed Mr Slowstache's belongings on to
the GUP-A, and the ship took off with a big SWOOSH.

Arriving at the sandy dunes of the beach, Barnacles looked around and smiled.
"It's ever so nice and warm – everyone seems to be enjoying the sun."

sunflower starfish

mussel beach

limpet

clam holes

sunbathing sea lion

sea urchin

barnacle

"I forgot how shallow the water is here.
An old turtle like me needs more shelter,"
Mr Slowstache fretted as he tucked into his shell. "Let's keep looking."

sand dollars

starfish beach party

kingfisher

pelican

anemone hat shop

vegetarian boiga

mud lobster towers

saltwater crocodile

crab clean-up crew

catfish kitchen

"How about this mangrove forest?" Dashi asked.
"The trees give cover to the animals and even drop fruit down for food."

flying fox

sleepy sloth

great egret

fish grooming

mudskipper

Shaking his head stubbornly, the turtle persisted,
"But I don't see any of my favourite seagrass!"

"Luckily, seagrass meadows grow right near mangroves," Peso announced cheerfully. "Look at those happy dugongs tending the fields."

possum

bandicoot

banjo ray

fish nurseries

pipefish

fiddler crab

seagrass band audience

sk

komodo dragon

black swan

cuttlefish

lawn mowing dugong

"The water is so murky here... not clean and clear like my old reef," fussed the turtle.

"Arrr, he's really picky – I need a holiday from this holiday!" Kwazii muttered.

Flipping his tail in frustration, Slowstache lamented, "I never realised how special my reef was until now. There's no other place quite like it!"

"If we can't find you a new home, we'll just have to figure out what's wrong with your old one," Barnacles said confidently. "Let's head back and solve this ghost reef mystery."

Returning to the city, the crew found Tweak
using the GUP-D to prop up a row of teetering buildings.

"Watch out!" the bunny shouted out with concern.
"The city is starting to fall. We need to do something fast!"

Just then, Shellington ran up to
the crew and exclaimed,
"Octonauts – while you were away,
I discovered something very fascinating!!
The reef isn't rock at all.
It's made up of thousands
of little creatures."

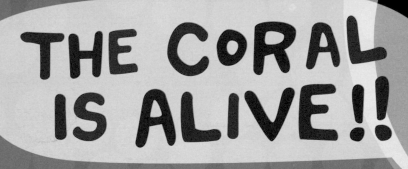

THE CORAL
IS ALIVE!!

"Does that mean they're not ghosts?"
Peso timidly asked.

Shellington shook his head and explained, "No, but they are cold and hungry. When I was studying the healthy reef outside town, I learned that each coral has algae inside that give it colour and help it make food."

"Algae are plants, and plants need light," Inkling added. "The buildings must be blocking out the sun and causing this coral to give up its algae."

"So that's why the reef turned white. Octonauts, we have to move these buildings!" Barnacles declared.

AH-HA!

News of the Octonauts' discovery spread quickly and animals from far and wide returned to help. Together, they lifted off pieces of city to uncover the coral beneath.

Everyone worked to build new homes *around* the coral instead of on top.
Slowly, the reef became colourful and healthy again.

"Thank you for solving this mystery – now I've learned that
we need to care for the reef just like it cares for us."
The turtle gratefully presented each of the crew
with a rock from his prized collection.
"For all your HARD work!" Slowstache added, with a wink.

SLOWSTACHE

The Octonauts laughed, and all agreed this was the greatest reef holiday ever!

MEET THE OCTONAUTS!

CAPTAIN BARNACLES BEAR

Brave Captain Barnacles is a polar bear extraordinaire and leader of the Octonauts crew. He is always the first to rush in and help when there is trouble. Besides adventuring, Barnacles enjoys playing his accordion and writing in his captain's log.

KWAZII KITTEN

Kwazii is a daredevil orange kitten from the mysterious Far East. This cat loves excitement and travelling to exotic places. Favourite pastimes include long baths, sword fighting and general swashbuckling.

PESO PENGUIN

Peso is the medic for the team. He enjoys putting bandages on cuts and tending to wounds. He's not too fond of scary things, but fortunately his big heart usually wins over monsters.

SHELLINGTON SEA OTTER

Shellington is a nerdy sea otter scientist who loves doing field research and lab work. He is easily distracted by rare plants and animals, which means he sometimes needs the other Octonauts to help him out of sticky situations.

TWEAK BUNNY

Tweak is the engineer for the Octopod. She keeps everything working properly below deck in the engine room and maintains the Octonauts' subs, GUP-A to GUP-E. Tweak loves all kinds of machinery and enjoys tinkering with strange contraptions that sometimes work in unexpected ways.

DASHI DOG

Dashi is the sweet dachshund dog who oversees operations in the Octopod control room and launch bay. She manages all ship traffic and ensures all the computers are in good working order. She also loves photographing all the wonderful underwater plants and animals.

PROFESSOR INKLING OCTOPUS

Professor Inkling is a brilliant Dumbo octopus oceanographer. He founded the Octonauts with the intention of furthering underwater research and preservation. Because of his size and delicate, big brain, he prefers to help out the team from the safety of the Octopod.

TUNIP THE VEGIMAL

Discovered by Dr Shellington, Tunip is one of many Vegimals, a special breed of underwater critter (part animal / part vegetable) who like to help out around the Octopod. Vegimals love to cook barnacle dishes: barnacle pasta, barnacle cakes, barnacle cookies...